Fiver's Dream

Diane Redmond

RED FOX

A Red Fox Book

Published by Random House Children's Books
20 Vauxhall Bridge Road, London SW1V 2SA

A division of The Random House Group Ltd
London Melbourne Sydney Auckland
Johannesburg and agencies throughout the world

www.watershipdown.net

Illustrations by County Studio, Leicester

1   3   5   7   9   10   8   6   4   2

Printed and bound in Italy by Lego SPA

THE RANDOM HOUSE GROUP Limited Reg. No. 954009

www.randomhouse.co.uk

ISBN 0 09 940315 3

This story represents scenes from the television series, Watership Down,
which is inspired by Richard Adams' novel of the same name.

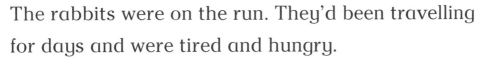

The rabbits were on the run. They'd been travelling
for days and were tired and hungry.

'I can't go any further,' wailed Pipkin, the smallest
of the group. 'I want to go home.'

'We can never go home again,' said Hazel. 'Our
warren has been destroyed.'

'So Fiver says!' said Hawkbit. 'But why
should we believe him – he's crazy!'

'Fiver has a gift,' said Hazel. 'His dreams
tell him what's going to happen. He
saw something terrible coming.
We had to leave!'

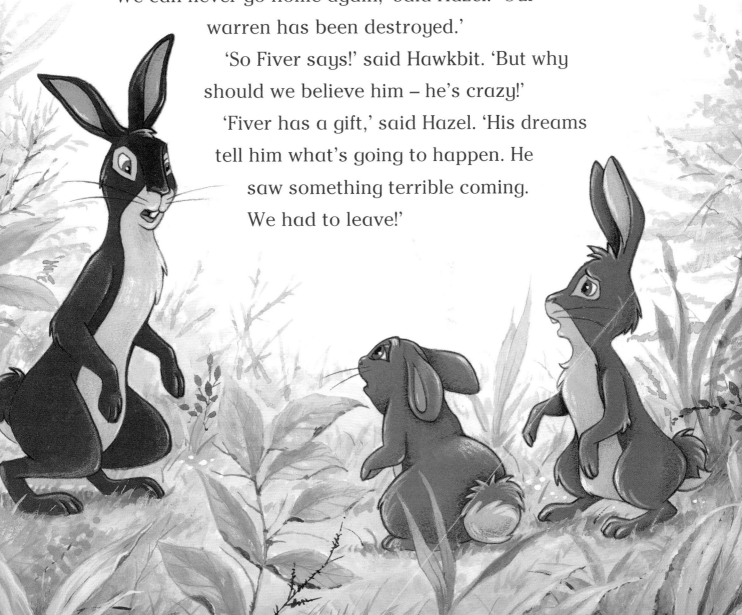

Fiver was sitting alone on a grassy bank. He knew his dream had changed their lives. He also knew there was a safe place where they could build a new warren and start again.

Hazel hopped across and sat beside his brother. 'What can you see, Fiver?' he asked.

Fiver closed his eyes. 'High hills. That's where we must go. That's where we'll find our new home.'

Hazel sighed. He wondered if it was far and if they'd all survive a long and dangerous journey.

'Woof! Woof! Woof!'

The sound of a dog barking made all the rabbits freeze.

Bigwig, a large buck, sniffed the air and swivelled his long ears. 'A dog's found our scent and is coming this way. Run quickly – now!'

The terrified rabbits darted into the thick ferns. The bigger rabbits ran easily, but Fiver and Pipkin were soon out of breath.

Hazel pulled Bigwig aside. 'Unless we distract the dog, the others won't have a chance,' he gasped.

'How?' asked Bigwig.

Hazel looked around. He spotted a hollow log. 'Follow me,' he said. 'Inside that log!'

Seconds later, the dog came bursting through the ferns. When he saw Hazel sitting on the log, he skidded to a halt. 'Grrrr!' he snarled, and charged at the rabbit.

But before the dog reached the log, Hazel ducked inside. A moment later Bigwig appeared at the other end.

The dog looked confused. He barked wildly, and then raced across to Bigwig.

While the rabbits teased him, the dog ran backwards and forwards. Then both rabbits disappeared. The dog was so angry he started to climb *inside* the log. He pushed in his big head and shoulders – and then he got stuck!

The rabbits saw their chance.

'Run!' yelled Hazel.

The dog tried to back out. He kicked wildly with his legs, but he couldn't move. Suddenly the log started to wobble! Then, with a bounce and a bump, it rolled down the bank and smashed into little pieces at the bottom.

Hazel and Bigwig found the other rabbits waiting for them on a river bank.

'Why have you stopped?' asked Bigwig.

'There's no way across!' cried Hawkbit.

Hazel stared at the wide river. 'We'll have to swim,' he said.

Pipkin looked terrified. 'I don't think I can,' he gulped.

The sound of the dog barking made the rabbits sit up.

'Into the river!' yelled Bigwig.

Hawkbit and Dandelion dived in, but Pipkin didn't move.

Fiver turned to Hazel. 'He won't make it!' he said desperately.

'Wait a minute! There *is* another way across!' cried Blackberry. She pointed to a log bobbing at the river's edge. 'Pipkin could float across.'

'That's a brilliant idea!' said Fiver.

Hazel and Bigwig looked confused. 'I'm missing something here,' said Bigwig.

'Quickly! On to the log, Pipkin,' said Fiver.

'I'm scared!' squeaked Pipkin.

Fiver hopped on beside him. 'Don't worry, I'll be with you,' he said.

'Hold tight!' called Blackberry, and pushed the log into the middle of the river, just as the dog came out of the woods.

'Swim!' cried Bigwig.

With a splash the rabbits jumped into the river and paddled hard. The dog didn't follow them – he was afraid of the water.

Dandelion and Hawkbit reached the other side first. They dragged themselves out of the river and collapsed on the bank.

'Safe at last,' breathed Dandelion.

'No, we're not!' said Hawkbit. 'Look! The current's sending Fiver and Pipkin back across the river. They're heading straight for the dog!'

The dog licked his lips as the log drifted towards him.

'What do we do now?' sobbed Pipkin.

'I don't know,' said Fiver. 'I'm sorry it had to end like this.'

Suddenly a loud voice gasped behind them. 'Nothing's ending while I'm around.'

'Bigwig!' yelled Pipkin and Fiver.

'I'm going to push, so hold tight!' he said.

The big rabbit put his nose to the log and turned it away from the waiting dog.

The dog was furious! He sprang forwards to bite Bigwig, but the bank was slippery and he went tumbling into the river!

As the dog splashed about in the water, Bigwig pushed the log towards the opposite bank. When they were safely there, Hawkbit and Dandelion helped the big rabbit out of the river. He was dripping with water and shook it all over them.

Fiver and Pipkin hopped quickly off the log. They looked at Bigwig with admiration.

'You saved us!' the young rabbits squealed.

'Nothing at all,' said Bigwig, who wasn't used to attention.

'Well done, everybody,' said Hazel. 'Now, come on, let's get moving!'

'But we're exhausted,' complained Hawkbit. 'Can't we rest here, just for a minute?'

'We'll have time to rest when we get where we're going,' said Hazel firmly.

Hawkbit scowled. 'We don't even *know* where we're going,' he grumbled.

Bigwig stamped his foot. 'You heard Hazel. Do as you're told, and hop to it!'

The weary rabbits set off once more on their journey. A long,
dangerous journey that they hoped would lead them to the
place in Fiver's dream – a safe home in the high hills.